First edition for the United States and Canada published
in 2010 by Barron's Educational Series, Inc.
First published in hardback in 2010 by Hodder Children's Books

Library of Congress Control No.: 2009932439

Date of Manufacture: December 2009
Manufactured by: WKT Shenzhen, China

All inquiries should be addressed to:
Barron's Educational Series, Inc.
250 Wireless Boulevard
Hauppauge, NY 11788
www.barronseduc.com

ISBN-13: 978-0-7641-6311-1
ISBN-10: 0-7641-6311-6

Printed in China
9 8 7 6 5 4 3 2 1

Lynne Rickards

Jacob O'Reilly Wants a Pet

Illustrated by
Lee Wildish

BARRON'S

Jacob O'Reilly had tried all he could
to convince Mom and Dad he'd be ever so good—
an absolute angel, the greatest son yet—
if only they'd let him have
one little pet!

He asked for a dog but Dad didn't want fleas.
He tried for a cat, but the fur made Mom sneeze.

He went through a list of small rodents for sale,
but the very idea turned Mom and Dad pale.

"If I'm not allowed gerbils
or hamsters or mice,
don't you think an iguana
would be rather nice?

He'd be awfully quiet
and eat all the bugs,
and never leave fur or
dead birds on the rugs...

Oh, PLEASE can I have a pet?"

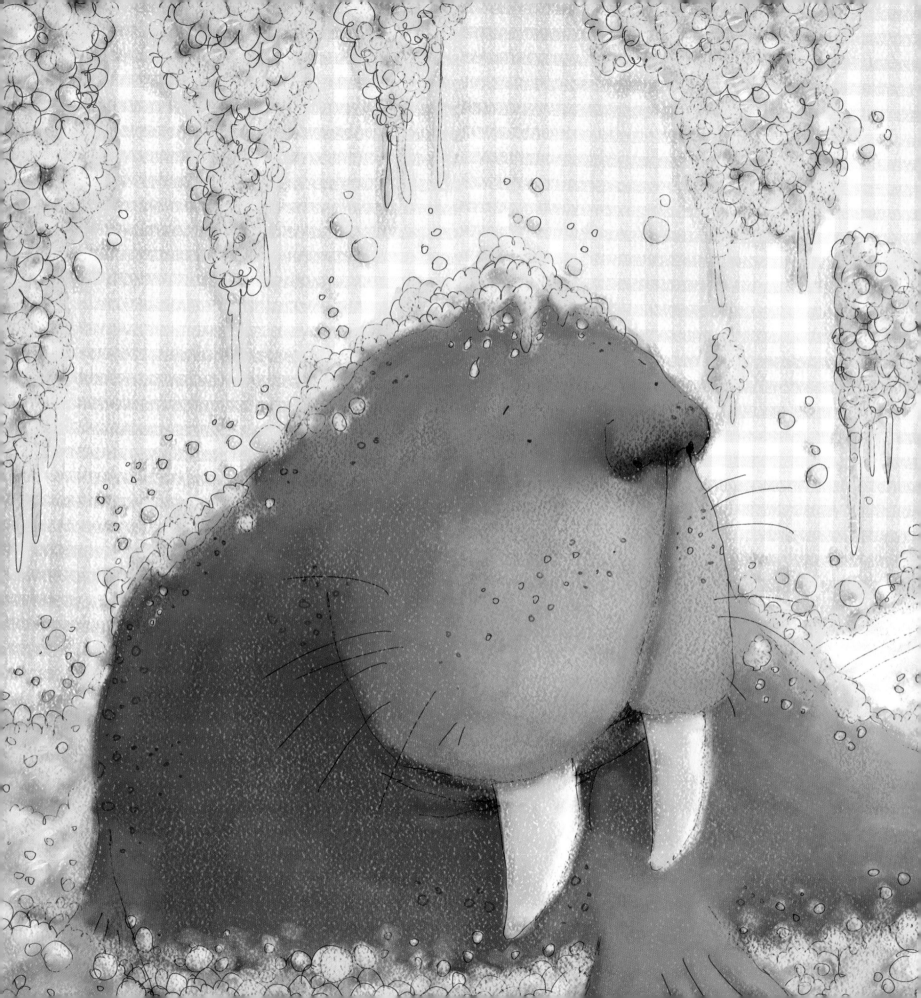

"A **walrus** would be an ideal sort of pet.
He could live in the bathtub to keep himself wet.
I'd comb out his whiskers and scrub his broad back,
and brush those big tusks when he finished a snack...

Oh, **PLEASE** can I have a pet?"

Well, Mom and Dad thought about all these suggestions while waiting for Jacob to run out of questions.

They pondered their choices and finally said, "Why not try your own pet-sitting business instead?"

The very next day, Jacob put up a sign:
"Come one and come all! Any number is fine!
I'll care for your pets while you take a nice break.
They'll have a great time here with
Pet-Sitter Jake!"

PET-SITTER "JAKE"

AT YOUR SERVICE!

In no time at all Jacob
had a full house—
four dogs and
five hamsters,
six cats, and one
mouse...

A python named Morris curled up on his bed,

two donkeys, five sheep, and one horse filled the shed,

the kitchen was hopping
with **rabbits** and **hares**,

and somebody's **zebra**
was blocking the stairs.

At feeding time Jacob was run off his feet—
some pets wanted salad, and some wanted meat.
They needed a hose-down when dinner was done,
and then it was time for a **marathon run!**

When two weeks were up and the owners came back,
the house had turned into a flea-bitten shack.
The minute the last pet whizzed off into town,
Pet-Sitter Jake went and pulled his sign down!

And that's when he noticed a rather fine snail,
Just sitting quietly there on a nail.
"Hello, there," smiled Jacob, "I don't think we've met."
And finally Jacob had found the right pet!